Linda Atnip

MIRANDA'S MAGIC GARDEN

Illustrated by Ann Rothan

Linda Atnip

MIRANDA'S MAGIC GARDEN

Illustrated by
Ann Rothan

Bluestar
Communications®

WOODSIDE, CALIFORNIA

11/04

Library of Congress Cataloging-in-Publication Data

Atnip, Linda, 1949-
Miranda's magic garden / Linda Atnip ; illustrated by Ann Rothan.
p. cm.
Summary: A contemporary fantasy in which a lonely little girl gains
friends and happiness when she listens to her dreams and helps the
plants grow a magic garden.
ISBN: 1-885394-21-7
[1. Dreams--Fiction. 2. Fantasy.] I. Rothan, Ann, ill.
II. Title.
PZ7.A86635Mi 1997
[E]--dc21   97-9928
                                                                                  CIP
                                                                                  AC

Edited by Jude Berman
Layout by Petra Michel
First Printing 1997
ISBN: 1-885394-21-7

Printed in China through Palace Press International

*This book is dedicated to the
memory of Margaret Sanders, my
first grade teacher at Mary Sharp
School, who inspired my love of
the written and spoken word.*

In the middle of a very large city, lived a lonely little girl named Miranda. The only place she had to play in was a small garden behind her apartment building. Since no other children lived nearby, Miranda spent many hours alone talking to the plants.

One day, she said to the sunflower, "I wish you could talk to me. My name is Miranda and I would love to be a flower and live outside. If I were a flower, I would make friends with all the other flowers growing near me."

Miranda began to pretend she was a sunflower, too. First she felt the sun warming her stalk. Then she imagined the wind lifting her petals into the air. She threw back her head and laughed as she thought a sunflower would.

Suddenly, Miranda felt a golden glow surrounding her. It seemed as if the sunshine inside the flower was beaming straight down upon her. She thought she heard the sunflower say, "We would like to be friends with you, too. But the human kingdom hasn't always treated us fairly."

Just in case the sunflower had really spoken, Miranda thought she had better answer. "What do you mean?" she asked.

"We are members of the plant kingdom," said the sunflower. "The members of our world are trees, flowers, vegetables, fruits and bushes. We are able to sense human thoughts. When we don't receive loving thoughts from humans, we feel lonely."

"You mean you feel like me?" asked Miranda.

"Often we do," answered the sunflower. "But you seem different, Miranda. We would like to know you better."

*M*iranda was very pleased. At last she had a friend. She began to dance about the garden, swinging her arms high and humming a song. She decided to call the tune "The March of the Sunflowers."

That night, Miranda dreamed of a beautiful meadow where wildflowers bloomed in brilliant colors. Row after row of sunflowers marched by. They were singing the same song she had been humming earlier.

We're the marching sunflowers Holding our heads high. Dancing, prancing, Having a great time.

We drink the light Shining from above And turn it into sunflowers To show you our love.

Come on, join in. Let's sing it again.

We're the marching sunflowers Holding our heads high. Dancing, prancing, Having a great time.

We drink the light Shining from above And turn it into sunflowers To show you our love.

We're the marching sunflowers Holding our heads high. Dancing, prancing, Reaching toward the sky.

The merry band was led by a wise, old woman beating a drum. She looked deeply into Miranda's eyes and said, "I've been waiting for you. I'm known as Keeper of the Earth. I live in the dream time where a rainbow bridge connects our two worlds. I hope you will visit me again soon."

The next morning, Miranda visited the garden and sat next to the sunflower. Closing her eyes, she began to daydream about the marching sunflowers.

Her daydream ended abruptly when she heard the sunflower speak out loud. "Hello," she said. "We are the devas that live in this garden."

"Are you a fairy?" asked Miranda.

"We are cousins of the fairy kingdom, but we live inside plants. In your world, cars need gas to run. In our world, we supply the energy to make plants grow. Here, let me show you what I mean."

Swirls of golden light, with flashes of green, burst forth from the sunflower, creating a halo around the plant. Slowly, she unfolded her leaves to reveal shiny green fingertips. When they were close enough to touch, the sunflower wrapped her brilliant halo around Miranda.

In that instant, the lonely little girl felt joy for the first time. Her heart raced, her mouth watered and tears ran down her cheeks. She could hardly believe her eyes. She could see a halo around each of the plants!

"Am I seeing double?" she asked.

"Miranda, right now, you can see inside our invisible world. We want to make you an honorary member of the plant kingdom. If you make us one special promise, we will share all our powers with you."

"What's that?" asked Miranda.

"Promise you will help us grow a magic garden," said the sunflower.

"I promise," answered Miranda.

That night, Miranda wondered how she would keep her promise. As she laid her head on her pillow, she asked herself, "What can I do to help my friends?" She thought and thought about the question, until finally she drifted off to sleep.

As she slept, Miranda had a familiar dream. She was lost in a forest during a raging storm. A giant grizzly bear was chasing her. The sound of her heart beating was as loud as the crackling thunder. Heavy rain pouring from the dark clouds completely soaked her clothing. She was cold, wet and afraid.

Miranda looked around frantically for something to hide under. But she couldn't find shelter anywhere. Finally, she saw a light in the distance. As she ran toward it, she heard a loud growl near her. The grizzly bear was getting closer! She turned to look back and tripped over a log. She tried to get up and run away, but it was too late. The bear's huge shadow covered everything.

Miranda gathered all her courage and stared directly into the grizzly's eyes. Instantly, the frightful bear melted away. In his place stood Keeper of the Earth. The old woman smiled, "Your bravery is about to be rewarded, Miranda. Hold out your hand."

Keeper of the Earth opened a small bag and poured a handful of brightly colored seeds into Miranda's outstretched hand. There were red, orange, yellow, green, blue, purple and white seeds. "Do you know what these are for?" she asked.

"The garden?" asked Miranda.

"Yes," answered Keeper of the Earth. "These are magic seeds from the dream time. If you water them and feed them with love each day, they will flower into a magical garden."

She helped Miranda gently place the seeds back in the bag. Then she said, "You are very brave, my child. You will work together with the plant kingdom. Listen to the devas. They will speak softly to you. Their words may come to you as pictures or even as feelings. Follow your heart and do whatever it tells you."

The next morning, a bright ray of sunshine fell across Miranda's bed, nudging her awake. She opened her eyes and saw an old leather pouch. She picked it up and peeked inside. It was full of rainbow-colored seeds. "How did this get here?" she asked herself. Then she remembered her dream.

Miranda jumped out of bed and ran outside shouting, "Look what Keeper of the Earth gave me!"

The sunflower smiled and said, "How wonderful, Miranda! However, you must keep in mind that these seeds do not belong to you. You are only their caretaker. No one owns anything that lives on the Earth." And she added, "We will grow this garden together. The seeds will let you know when it's the right time to plant them."

A week later, Miranda had an idea about how the rows should be planted. A picture formed in her mind of four plants growing in each row, in a checkerboard pattern. She picked up her tiny trowel and began to dig.

As she dropped each seed into its new home, Miranda gave it a drink of water. "Grow well, little seed," she said. "And, please, blossom."

Time passed swiftly as Miranda lovingly tended her garden. One morning she looked out her bedroom window and saw tiny shoots poking out of the ground. Little green leaves danced in the wind. Amazed at the new life springing up all around her, Miranda ran into the garden.

"The seeds are alive! They're alive," she shouted.

During the next month, the plants grew larger and larger until an unexpected visitor arrived—Mr. Mole.

The small, brown, furry creature burrowed holes all over the garden.

Miranda tried to catch Mr. Mole with her bare hands. But he was much too slippery. She watched helplessly while he dug up the daffodil and the iris. That night, as she went to bed, Miranda wondered what she could possibly do to save the garden.

A little while later, a blazing sun woke Miranda. She found herself standing on a path of golden bricks. Just ahead, the seven colors of the rainbow arched across the most beautiful stream she had ever seen. She could see inside the colors, so she knew the bridge wasn't solid. Yet, she felt no fear as she stepped onto it.

A puff of smoke announced the arrival of Keeper of the Earth. "Miranda, what an extraordinary child you are! Never before has anyone entered the dream time without a guide. Yet, here you are! What can I do for you?"

"Mr. Mole has been digging up all the plants in the magic garden!" Miranda cried. "Can you please help me find a way to make him stop?"

"Of course, my child," replied Keeper of the Earth. "First make friends with Mr. Mole. Then you can suggest that he move his digging to another place. Find him a special place to dig that he knows is his very own. By doing it this way, you can keep him as a friend."

The next morning, Miranda began her search for a new home for Mr. Mole.

Soon she noticed an empty lot behind the garden. In the lot was a small dirt tunnel that she thought would be perfect for Mr. Mole.

Miranda told all the plants about her dream and they agreed to help her guide the mole to his new home. The plan was hatched. First she led the garden quartet in singing "The March of the Sunflowers." The plants sang in perfect harmony. Their sounds were so beautiful that Mr. Mole began to follow along.

Then like a pied piper, Miranda zigzagged through the garden, guiding Mr. Mole toward the tunnel. He was having so much fun, he even swished his tail in time with the music.

Miranda led Mr. Mole directly to the mouth of the tunnel. When he saw the hole in the ground, his curiosity overwhelmed him and he dove straight in.

r. Mole was delighted with his new home. A vast network of tunnels stretched underground for him to explore. Now, he could continue digging without damaging the garden.

By midsummer, the sunflowers had grown so high that they were ten times taller than Miranda! The hibiscus, the lilies and the daisies were in full bloom, creating a living kaleidoscope of color.

One of Miranda's neighbors took a photo of the little girl standing beside her gigantic sunflowers. He showed the photo to a reporter from the neighborhood newspaper. No one could believe that a small child had grown this garden!

The reporter came out to interview her. "What is your secret, Miranda?" he asked. "How did you get the sunflowers to grow so tall?"

"We grew the garden together. Plants know what they need to grow. If you listen to them with your inner ears, you can hear their voices. The flowers just want to be loved and cared for," said the young philosopher.

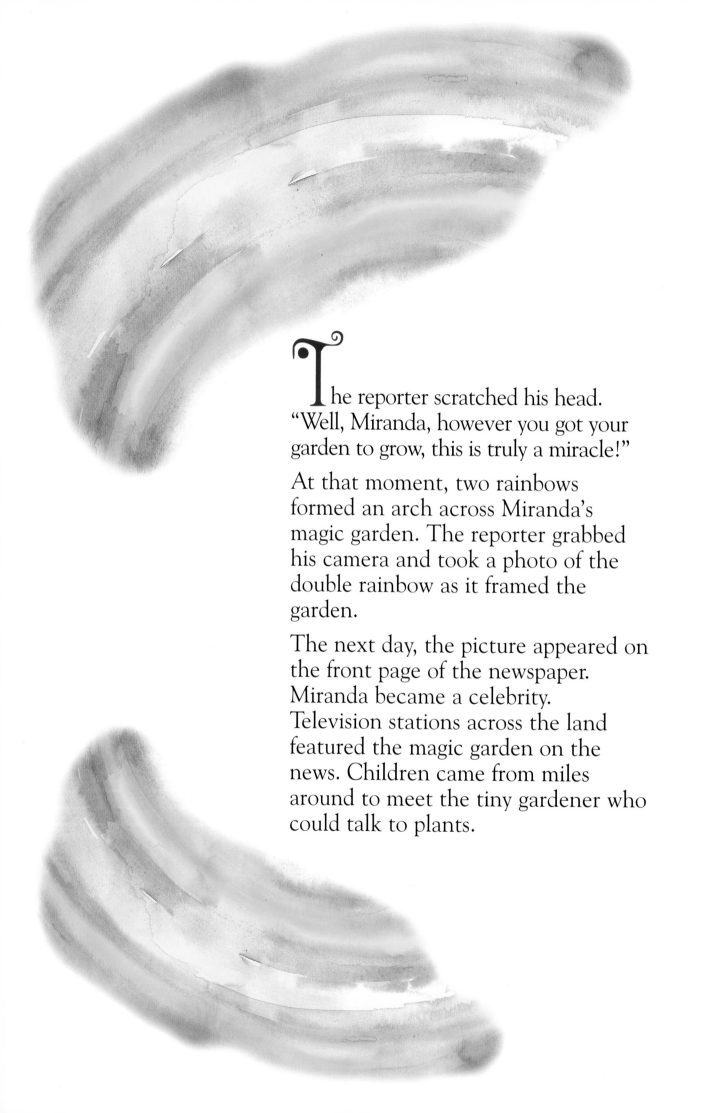

The reporter scratched his head. "Well, Miranda, however you got your garden to grow, this is truly a miracle!"

At that moment, two rainbows formed an arch across Miranda's magic garden. The reporter grabbed his camera and took a photo of the double rainbow as it framed the garden.

The next day, the picture appeared on the front page of the newspaper. Miranda became a celebrity. Television stations across the land featured the magic garden on the news. Children came from miles around to meet the tiny gardener who could talk to plants.

iranda's life grew as rich as the soil in the magic garden. She made many new friends. She introduced them to the devas and to her old friend, Mr. Mole.

All over the city, children followed Miranda's example and planted their own magic gardens. The city began to flourish. It grew greener and cleaner, thanks to its young crop of gardeners.

EPILOGUE

Dreams are one of life's greatest mysteries. They can yield incredible gifts with just a little digging. By teaching children to look at their dreams as treasure hunts, you can profoundly enrich their—as well as your—lives.

As a parent, all you need to get started is a sharing time, preferably in the morning when your child's dreams are still fresh in mind. You may want to keep a dream journal together, in which you write down the content of the dreams. Then your child can illustrate them, or act them out.

When your child shares a dream with you, you can make up a game in which you try to connect the dots between the dream and the waking world. You can also make a list of supportive dream guides that your child can call on for help during nightmares.

If your child has a recurring nightmare, like Miranda's dream of being chased by a grizzly bear, teach your child to take action and confront the monster. Let the child know he or she has the power to change any aspect of the dream.

To foster happier dreams, try reading aloud just before bedtime. Pick stories in which the characters have joyful adventures. Or tell your child a story about a happy dream experience that you made up yourself.

These are just a few ideas to get you started. By following my visionary muse, I have come to realize there is no greater gift that we can give to our children than to listen to their dreams and encourage them to act upon them. It is my sincerest wish that this book will inspire you to engage in dream play with the children in your life and make it an integral part of every day. The rewards your child will reap will be immeasurable.

Linda Atnip
Los Angeles, January 18, 1997

ABOUT THE AUTHOR

Photography by Roch Doran

Miranda's Magic Garden is a contemporary fantasy inspired by the two loves of the author, Linda Atnip: the physical world of nature and the ethereal world of dreams. To bring these forces into balance, she created characters who are grounded in each reality, and based their actions on volumes of research and her own dream time experiences.

In her dynamic career spanning twenty years, author, performance and recording artist Linda Atnip has always been a communications visionary who paints pictures with words. A native of Winchester, Tennessee, she graduated from Florida State University with a degree in Broadcast Journalism and worked as a television news reporter and entertainment editor before relocating to the West Coast and devoting herself full time to a writing and performing career.

For the past ten years, Linda's dream life has been a very fertile ground that directed her to write two collections of poetry, *When the Heart Sings* and *Earth's Sacred Chant*; a one-woman show, *The Dream Voyage*, and this children's book, *Miranda's Magic Garden*. Her nightly excursions are not random events, but a series of carefully orchestrated messages leading her toward a life's work of inspiring others to live their dreams.

The author, Linda Atnip, is shown portraying Woman of the Doves, a Rainbow Warrior, in "The Dream Voyage," an original one-woman show depicting dream guides who challenge the audience to face their innermost fears and create their greatest dream for humanity. The multi-media performance piece which blends spoken word, voice overs, music, dance, movement and audio-visuals was presented at Barnsdale Art Park Gallery Theatre in Hollywood by the City of Los Angeles Cultural Affairs Department.

ABOUT THE ILLUSTRATOR

Ann Rothan works as an illustrator, teacher, visionary and futurist. Though Ann's art is figurative in style, her paintings are symbolic in meaning. Unveiling these symbols reveals the deeper, hidden teachings of her work. She illustrates for magazines, publishers and recording artists. Ann's work can be seen in galleries in Florida and Oregon.